THE BLACK MAN

THE BLACK MAN

EMILY ANDRADE CRAVALHO

aldivan teixeira torres

CONTENTS

1   1

CHAPTER 1

"The Black Man"
Emily Andrade Cravalho

The BLACK MAN

By: **Emily Andrade Cravalho**
2020- Emily *Andrade Cravalho*
All rights reserved
Series: The Perverted Sisters

This book, including all its parts, is copyrighted and cannot be reproduced without the permission of the author, resold or transferred.

Emily Andrade Cravalho, born in Brazil, is a literary artist. Promises with his writings to delight the public and lead him to the delights of pleasure. After all, sex is one of the best things there is.

Dedication and thanks

I dedicate this erotic series to all sex lovers and perverts like me. I hope to meet the expectations of all insane minds. I start this work here with the conviction that Amelinha, Belinha and their friends will make history. Without further ado, a warm hug to my readers.

Good reading and lots of fun.

With affection, the author.

Presentation

Amelinha and Belinha are two sisters born and raised in the interior of Pernambuco. Daughters of farming fathers knew early on how to face the fierce difficulties of the country life with a smile on their face. With this, they were reaching their personal conquests. The first is a public finance auditor and the other, less intelligent, is a municipal teacher of basic education in Arcoverde.

Although they be happy professionally, the two have a serious chronic problem regarding relationships because never found their prince charming, which is every woman's dream. The eldest, Belinha, came to live with a man for a while. However, it was betrayed what generated in its small heart irreparable traumas. She was forced to part ways and promised herself never to suffer again because of a man. Amelinha, poor thing, she can't even get ourselves engaged. Who wants to marry Amelinha? She is a cheeky brunette, skinny, medium height, honey-colored eyes, medium butt, breasts like watermelon, chest defined beyond a captivating smile. No one knows what her real problem is, or rather both.

In relation to their interpersonal relationship, they are very close to sharing secrets between them. Since Belinha was betrayed by a scoundrel, Amelinha took the pains of her sister and also set out to play with men. The two became a dynamic duo known as the "Perverted Sisters". Despite that, men love being their toys. This is because there is nothing better than loving Belinha and Amelinha even for a moment. Shall we get to know their stories together?

The black man

Amelinha and Belinha as well as great professionals and lovers, are beautiful and rich women integrated into social networks. In addition to the sex itself, they also seek to make friends.

Once, a man entered the virtual chat. His nickname was "Black Man". At this moment, she soon trembled because she loved black men. Legend has it that they have an undisputed charm.

—Hello, beautiful! - You called the blessed black man.

—Hello, all right? - Answered the intriguing Belinha.

—All great. Have a good night!

—Good night. I love black people!

—This has touched me deeply now! But is there a special reason for this? What is your name?

—Well, the reason is my sister and I like men, if you know what I mean. As far as the name goes, even though this is a very private environment, I have nothing to hide. My name is Belinha. Pleased to meet you.

—The pleasure is all mine. My name is Flavius, and I'm a very nice!

—I felt firmness in his words. You mean my intuition is right?

—I can't answer that now because that would end the whole mystery. What's your sister's name?

—Her name is Amelinha.

—Amelinha! Beautiful name! Can you describe yourself physically?

—I'm blonde, tall, strong, long hair, big butt, medium breasts, and I have a sculptural body. And you?

—Black color, one meter and eighty centimeters high, strong, spotted, arms and legs thick, neat, singed hair and defined faces.

—Ouch! Ouch! You turn me on!

—Don't worry about it. Who knows me, never forgets.

—You want to drive me crazy now?

—Sorry about that, baby! It's just to add a little charm to our conversation.

—How old are you?

—Twenty-five years and yours?

—I am thirty-eight years old and my sister thirty-four. Despite the age difference, we're very close. In childhood, we united to overcome difficulties. When we were teenagers, we shared our dreams. And now, in adulthood, we share our achievements and frustrations. I can't live without her.

—Great! This feeling of yours is very beautiful. I'm getting the urge to meet you both. Is she as naughty as you?

—In a good way, she's the best at what she does. Very smart, beautiful and polite. My advantage is I'm smarter.

—But I don't see a problem in this. I like both.

—Do you really like it? You know, Amelinha is a special woman. Not because she's my sister, but because she has a giant heart. I feel a little sorry for her because she never got a groom. I know her dream is to get married. She joined me in an uprising because I was betrayed by my companion. Since then, we seek only fast relationships.

—I totally understand. I'm also a pervert. However, I have no special reason. I just want to enjoy my youth. You seem like great people.

—Thank you very much. Are you really from Arcoverde?

—Yeah, I'm from downtown. And you?

—From the San Cristóbal neighborhood.

—Great. Do you live alone?

—Yes. Near the bus station.

—Can you get a visit from a man today?

—We'd love to. But you have to handle both. Okay?

—Don't you worry, love. I can handle up to three.

—Ah, yes! True!

—I'll be right there. can you explain the location?

—Yes. It'll be my pleasure.

—I know where it is. I'm coming up there!

The Black man left the room and Belinha also. She took advantage of it and moved to the kitchen where she met her sister. Amelinha was washing the dirty dishes for dinner.

—Good night to you, Amelinha. You will not believe. Guess who's coming over?

—I have no idea, sister. Who?

—The Flavius. I met him in the virtual chat room. He'll be our entertainment today.

—What does he look like?

—It is Black Man. Did you ever stop and think that it might be nice? The poor man doesn't know what we're capable of!

—It really is, sister! Let's finish him off.

—He will fall, with me! - Said Belinha.

—No! It will be with me-Replied Amelinha.

—One thing is certain: With one of us he will fall-Belinha concluded.

—It is true! How about we get everything ready in the bedroom?

—Good idea. I'll help you out!

The two insatiable dolls went to the room leaving everything organized for the arrival of the male. As soon as they finish, they hear the bell ring.

—Is it him, sister? - Asked Amelinha.

—Let's check it out together! - He invited Belinha.

—Come on! Amelinha agreed.

Step by step, the two women passed the bedroom door, passed the dining room and then arrived in the living room. They walked to the door. When they open it, they encounter Flavius's charming and manly smile.

—Good night! All right? I am the Flavius.

—Good night. You are most welcome. I'm Belinha who was talking to you on the computer and this sweet girl next to me is my sister.

—Nice to meet you, Flavius! - Amelinha said.

—Nice to meet you. Can I come in?

—Sure! - The two women answered at the same time.

The stallion had access to the room by observing every detail of the decor. What was going on in that boiling mind? He was especially touched by each of those female specimens. After a brief moment, he looked deeply into the eyes of the two whores saying:

—Are you ready for what I've come to do?

—Ready-Affirmed the lovers!

The trio stopped hard and walked a long way to the larger room of the house. By closing the door, they were sure heaven would go to hell in a matter of seconds. Everything was perfect: The arrangement of the towels, the sex toys, the porn film playing on the ceiling television and the romantic music vibrant. Nothing could take away the pleasure of a great evening.

The first step is to sit by the bed. The black man started taking off his clothes of the two women. Their lust and thirst for sex was so great that they caused a little anxiety in those sweet ladies. He was taking off his shirt showing the thorax and abdomen well worked out by the daily workout at the gym. Your average hairs all over this region have drawn sighs from the girls. Afterwards, he took off his pants allowing the view of his Box underwear consequently showing his volume and masculinity. At this time, he allowed them to touch the organ, making it more erect. With no secrets, he threw his underwear away showing everything God gave him.

He was twenty-two centimeters long, fourteen centimeters in diameter enough to drive them crazy. Without wasting time, they fell on him. They started with the foreplay. While one swallowed her cock in her mouth, the other licked the scrotum bags. In this operation, it's been three minutes. Long enough to be completely ready for sex.

Then he began penetration into one and then into the other without preference. The frequent pace of the shuttle caused groans, screams, and multiple orgasms following the act. It was thirty minutes of vaginal sex. Each one half the time. Then they concluded with oral and anal sex.

The fire

It was a cold, dark and rainy night in the capital of all the backwoods of Pernambuco. There were moments when the front winds reached 100 kilometers per hour scaring the poor sisters Amelinha and Belinha. The two perverted sisters met in the living room of their simple residence in the São Cristóvão neighborhood. With nothing to do, they talked happily about general things.

—Amelinha, how was your day at the farm office?

—The same old thing: I organized the tax planning of the tax and customs administration, managed the payment of taxes, worked in the prevention and combat of tax evasion. It's hard work and boring. But rewarding and well paid. And you? How was your routine in school? - Asked Amelinha.

—In class, I passed the contents guiding the students in the best way possible. I corrected the mistakes and took two cell phones of students who were disturbing the class. I also gave classes in behavior, posture, dynamics and useful advice. Anyway, besides being a teacher, I'm their mother. Proof of this is that, at intermission, I infiltrated the class of students and ,together with them, we played hopscotch, hula hoop, hit and run. In my view, school is our second home and we must look after the friendships and human connections that we have from it-Belinha replied.

—Brilliant, my little sister. Our works are great because they provide important emotional and interaction constructions between people. No human can live in isolation, let alone without psychological and financial resources- analyzed Amelinha.

—I agree. Work is essential to us as it makes us independent of the prevailing sexist empire in our society-said Belinha.

—Exactly. We will continue in our values and attitudes. Man is only good in bed- Amelinha observed.

—Speaking of men, what did you think of Christian? - Belinha asked.

—He lived up to my expectations. After such an experience, my instincts and my mind always ask for more generating internal dissatisfaction. What is your opinion? - Asked Amelinha.

—It was good, but I also feel like you: incomplete. I'm dry of love and sex. I want more and more. What do we have for today? - Said Belinha.

—I'm out of ideas. The night is cold, dark and dark. Do you hear the noise outside? There's a lot of rain, strong winds, lightning and thunder. I'm scared! - Said Amelinha.

—Me too! - Belinha confessed.

At this moment, a thunderous thunderbolt is heard throughout Arcoverde. Amelinha jumps in the lap of Belinha who screams of pain and despair. At the same time, electricity is lacking, making them both desperate.

—What now? What will we do Belinha? - Asked Amelinha.

—Get off me, bitch! I'll get the candles! - Said Belinha. Belinha gently pushed her sister to the side of the couch as she groped the walls to get to the kitchen. As the house is relatively small, it does not take long to complete this operation. Using tact, he takes the candles in the cupboard and lights them with the matches strategically placed on top of the stove.

With the lighting of the candle, she calmly returns to the room where he meets his sister with a mysterious smile wide open on his face. What was she up to?

—You can vent, sister! I know you're thinking something- Said Belinha .

—What if we called the city fire department warning of a fire? Said Amelinha.

—Let me get this straight. You want to invent a fictional fire to lure these men? What if we get arrested? - Belinha was afraid.

—My colleague! I'm sure they'll love the surprise. What better do they have to do on a dark and dull night like this? - said Amelinha.

—You are right. They'll thank you for the fun. We will break the fire that consumes us from the inside. Now, the question comes: Who will have the courage to call them? - asked Belinha.

—I am very shy. I leave this task to you, my sister- Said Amelinha

—Always me. Okay. Whatever happens happens- Belinha concluded.

Getting up from the couch, Belinha goes to the table in the corner where the mobile is installed. She calls the fire department's emergency number and is waiting to be answered. After a few touches, he hears a deep, firm voice speaking from the other side.

—Good night. This is the fire department. What do you want?

—My name is Belinha. I live in the São Cristóvão neighborhood here in Arcoverde. My sister and I are desperate with all this rain. When electricity went out here in our house, caused a short circuit, starting to set the objects on fire. Luckily, my sister and I went out. The fire is slowly consuming the house. We need the help of the firemen- said distressed the girl.

—Take it easy, my friend. We'll be there soon. Can you give detailed information about your location? - Asked the fireman on duty.

—My house is exactly on Central Avenue, third house on the right. Is that okay with you guys?

—I know where it is. We'll be there in a few minutes. Be calm- Said the fireman.

—We are waiting. Thank you! - Thank you Belinha.

Returning to the couch with a wide grin, the two of them let off their pillows and snorted with the fun they were doing. However, this is not recommended to do unless they were two whores like them.

About ten minutes later, they heard a knock on the door and went to answer it. When they opened the door, they faced three magical faces, each with its characteristic beauty. One was black, six feet tall, legs and arms medium. Another was dark, one meter and ninety tall, muscular and sculptural. A third was white, short, thin, but very fond. The white boy wants to introduce himself:

—Hi, ladies, good night! My name is Roberto. This man next door is called Matthew and the brown man, Philip. What are your names and where is the fire?

—I'm Belinha, I spoke to you on the phone. This brunette here is my sister Amelinha. Come in and I'll explain it to you.

—Okay - They took in the three firemen at the same time.

The quintet entered the house and everything seemed normal because the electricity had returned. They settle on the sofa in the living room along with the girls. Suspicious, they make conversation.

—The fire is over, is it? - Matthew asked.

—Yes. We already control it thanks to a great effort- explained Amelinha.

—Pity! I've been wanting to work. There at the barracks the routine is so monotonous-said Felipe.

—I have an idea. How about working in a more pleasurable way? - Belinha suggested.

—You mean that you are what I think? - Questioned Felipe.

—Yes. We're single women who love pleasure. In the mood for fun? - asked Belinha.

—Only if you go now- answered black man.

—I'm in too- confirmed the Brown Man.

—Wait for me- The white boy is available.

—So, let's- Said the girls.

The quintet entered the room sharing a double bed. Then began the sex orgy. Belinha and Amelinha took turns to attend the pleasure of the three firefighters. Everything seemed magical and there was no better feeling than being with them. With varied gifts, they experienced sexual and positional variations creating a perfect picture.

The girls seemed insatiable in their sexual ardor what drove those professionals mad. They went through the night having sex and the pleasure seemed never to end. They didn't leave until they got an urgent call from work. They quit and went to answer the police report. Even so, they would never forget that wonderful experience alongside the "Perverted Sisters".

Medical consultation

It dawned on the beautiful outback capital. Usually, the two perverted sisters were waking up early. However, when they got up, they did not feel well. While Amelinha kept sneezing, her sister Belinha felt a little suffocated. These facts probably came from the previous night in Virginia War Square where they drank, kissed on the mouth and snorted harmoniously in the serene night.

As they were not feeling well and without strength for anything, they sat on the couch religiously thinking about what to do because professional commitments were waiting to be resolved.

–What do we do, sister? I'm totally out of breath and exhausted- Said Belinha.

–Tell me about it! I have a headache and I'm starting to get a virus. We are lost! - Said Amelinha.

–But I don't think that's a reason to miss work! People depend on us! - Said Belinha

–Calm down, let's not panic! How about we join the nice? - Suggested Amelinha.

–Don't tell me you're thinking what I'm thinking.... - Belinha was amazed.

—That's right. Let's go to the doctor together! It will be a great reason to miss work and who knows does not happen what we want! - Said Amelinha

—Great idea! So, what are we waiting for? Let's get ready! - asked Belinha.

—Come on! - Amelinha agreed.

The two went to their respective enclosures. They were so excited about the decision; they didn't even look sick. Was it all just their invention? Forgive me, reader, let's not think badly of our dear friends. Instead, we will accompany them in this exciting new chapter of their lives.

In the bedroom, they bathed in their suites, put on new clothes and shoes, combed their long hair, put on a French perfume and then went to the kitchen. There, they smashed eggs and cheese filling two loaves of bread and ate with a chilled juice. Everything was very delicious. Even so, they didn't seem to feel it because the anxiety and nervousness in front of the doctor's appointment were gigantic.

With everything ready, they left the kitchen to exit the house. With each step they took, their little hearts throbbed with emotion thinking in a completely new experience. Blessed be they all! Optimism took hold of them and was something to be followed by others!

On the outside of the house, they go to the garage. Opening the door in two attempts, they stand in front of the modest red car. Despite their good taste in cars, they preferred the popular ones to the classics for fear of the common violence present in almost all Brazilian regions.

Without delay, the girls enter the car giving the exit gently and then one of them closes the garage returning to the car immediately after. Who drives is Amelinha with experience already ten years. Belinha is not yet allowed to drive.

The very short route between their home and the hospital is done with safety, harmony and tranquility. At that moment, they had the false feeling that they could do anything. Contradictorily, they were afraid of his cunning and freedom. They themselves were surprised by the actions taken. It wasn't for anything less that they were called slutty good bastards!

Arriving at the hospital, they scheduled the appointment and waited to be called. In this time interval, they took advantage of making a snack and exchanged messages through the mobile application with their dear sexual servants. More cynical and cheerful than these, it was impossible to be!

After a while, it's their turn to be seen. Inseparable, they enter the care office. When this happens, doctor almost have a heart attack. In front of them was a rare piece of a man: A tall blond, one meter and ninety centimeters tall, bearded, hair forming a ponytail, muscular arms and breasts, natural faces with an angelic look. Even before they could draft a reaction, he invites:

–Sit down, both of you!

–Thank you! - They said both.

The two have time to make a quick analysis of the environment: In front of the service table, the doctor, the chair in which he was sitting and behind a closet. On the right side, a bed. On the wall, expressionist paintings by author Cândido Portinari depicting the man from the countryside. The atmosphere is very cozy leaving the girls at ease. The atmosphere of relaxation is broken by the formal aspect of the consultation.

–Tell me what you're feeling, girls!

That sounded informal to the girls. How sweet was that blond man! It must have been delicious to eat.

–Headache, indisposition and virus! - Told Amelinha.

–I'm breathless and tired! - He claimed Belinha.

—It's ok! Let me take a look! Lie down on the bed! - The Doctor asked.

The whores were barely breathing at this request. The professional made them take off part of their clothes and felt them in various parts which caused chills and cold sweats. Realizing that there was nothing serious with them, the attendant joked:

—It all looks perfect! What do you want them to be afraid of? An injection in the ass?

—I love it! If it is a large and thick injection even better! - Said Belinha.

—Will you apply slowly, love? - Said Amelinha.

—You are already asking too much! - Noted the clinician.

Carefully closing the door, he falls on the girls like a wild animal. First, he takes the rest of the clothes off the bodies. This sharpens his libido even more. By being completely naked, he admires for a moment those sculptural creatures. Then it's his turn to show off. He makes sure they take off their clothes. This increases the interplay and intimacy between the group.

With everything ready, they begin the preliminaries of sex. Using the tongue in sensitive parts like the anus, the ass and the ear the blonde causes mini pleasure orgasms in both women. Everything was going fine even when someone kept knocking on the door. No way out, he has to answer. He walks a little and opens the door. In doing so, he comes across the on-call nurse: a slender mulatto, with thin legs and very low.

—Doctor, I have a question about a patient's medication: is it five or three hundred milligrams of Clotrimazole? - Asked Roberto showing a recipe.

—Five hundred! - Confirmed Alex.

At this moment, the nurse saw the feet of the naked girls who were trying to hide. Laughed inside.

—Joking around a little bit, huh, Doc? Don't even call your friends!

—Excuse me! You want to join the gang?

—I would love to!

—Then come!

The two entered the room closing the door behind them. More than quickly, the mulatto took off his clothes. Totally naked, he showed his long, thick, veiny mast as a trophy. Belinha was delighted and was soon giving him oral sex. Alex also demanded that Amelinha do the same with him. After oral, they started anal. In this part, Belinha found it very difficult to hold on to the nurse's monster cock. But once it entered the hole, their pleasure was enormous. On the other hand, they didn't feel any difficulty because their penis was normal.

Then they had vaginal sex in various positions. The movement of back and forth in the cavity caused hallucinations in them. After this stage, the four united in a group sex. It was the best experience in which the remaining energies were spent. Fifteen minutes later, they were both sold out. For the sisters, sex would never end, but good as they were respected the frailty of those men. Not wanting to disturb their work, they quit taking the certificate of justification of the work and their personal phone. They left completely composed without arousing anyone's attention during the hospital crossing.

Arriving at the parking lot, they entered the car and started the way back. Happy as they are, they were already thinking about their next sexual mischief. The perverted sisters were really something!

Private Lesson

It was an afternoon like any other. Newcomers from work, the perverted sisters were busy with household chores. After finishing all the tasks, they gathered in the room to rest a little. While Amelinha read a book, Belinha used the mobile internet to browse her favorite websites.

At some point, the second screams out loud in the room, which frightens her sister.

-What is it, girl? Are you crazy? - Asked Amelinha.

-I just accessed the website of contests having a grateful surprise- informed Belinha.

-Tell me more!

-Registrations of the federal regional court are open. Let's do?

-Good call, my sister! What is the salary?

-More than ten thousand initial dolars.

-Very good! My job is better. However, I will make the contest because I am preparing myself looking for other events. It will serve as an experiment.

-You do very well! You encourage me. Now, I don't know where to begin. Can you give me tips?

-Buy a virtual course, ask a lot of questions on the test sites, do and redo previous tests, write summaries, watch tips and download good materials on the internet among other things.

-Thank you! I'll take all this advice! But I need something more. Look, sister, since we have money, how about we pay for a private lesson?

-I hadn't thought of that. That's a good idea! Do you have any suggestions for a competent person?

-I have a very competent teacher here from Arcoverde in my phone contacts. Look at his picture!

Belinha gave her sister her cell phone. Seeing the boy's picture, she was ecstatic. Besides handsome, he was smart! It would be a perfect victim of the pair joining the useful to the pleasant.

-What are we waiting for? Go get him, sister! We need to study soon. - Amelinha said.

-You got it! - Belinha accepted.

Getting up from the couch, she began to dial the numbers of the phone on the number pad. Once the call is made, it will only take a few moments to be answered.

-Hello. You all right?

-It's all great, Renato.

-Send out the orders.

-I was surfing the Internet when I discovered that applications for the federal regional court competition are open. I named my mind immediately as a respectable teacher. Do you remember the school season?

-I remember that time well. Good times those who don't come back!

-That's right! Do you have time to give us a private lesson?

-What a conversation, young lady! For you I always have time! What date do we set?

-Can we do it tomorrow at 2:00 ? We need to get started!

-Of course I do! With my help, I humbly say that the chances of passing increase incredibly.

-I'm sure of it!

-How good! You can expect me at 2:00.

-Thank you very much! See you tomorrow!

-See you later!

Belinha hung up the phone and sketched a smile for his companion. Suspecting the answer, Amelinha asked:

-How did it go?

-He accepted. Tomorrow at 2:00 he'll be here.

-How good! Nerves are killing me!

-Just take it easy, sister! It's gonna be okay.

-Amen!

-Shall we prepare dinner? I am already hungry!

-Well remembered.!

The pair went from the living room to the kitchen where in a pleasant environment talked, played, cooked among other activities. They were exemplary figures of sisters united by pain and loneliness. The fact that they were bastards in sex only qualified them even more. As you all know, the Brazilian woman has warm blood.

Soon after, they were fraternizing around the table, thinking about life and its vicissitudes.

-Eating this delicious chicken stroganoff, I remember the black man and the firemen! Moments that never seem to pass! - Belinha said!

- Tell me about it! Those guys are delicious! Not to mention the nurse and the doctor! I loved it too! - Remembered Amelinha!

-True enough, my sister! Having a beautiful mast any man becomes pleasant! May the feminists forgive me!

-We don't need to be so radical...!

The two laugh and continue to eat the food on the table. For a moment, nothing else mattered. They seemed to be alone in the world and that qualified them as Goddesses of beauty and love. Because the most important thing is to feel good and have self-esteem.

Confident in themselves, they continue in the family ritual. At the end of this stage, they surf the internet, listen to music on the living room stereo, watch soap operas and, later, a porn film. This rush leaves them breathless and tired forcing them to go to rest in their respective rooms. They were eagerly waiting for the next day.

It won't be long before they fall into a deep sleep. Apart from nightmares, night and dawn take place within the normal range. As soon as dawn comes, they get up and begin to follow the normal routine: Bath, breakfast, work, return home, bath, lunch, nap and move to the room where they wait for the scheduled visit.

When they hear knocking at the door, Belinha gets up and goes to answer. In doing so, he comes across the smiling teacher. This caused him good internal satisfaction.

-Welcome back, my friend! Ready to teach us?

-Yes, very, very ready! Thanks again for this opportunity! - Said Renato.

-Let's go in! - Said Belinha.

The boy did not think twice and accepted the request of the girl. He greeted Amelinha and on her signal, sat on the couch. His first attitude was to take off the black knitted blouse because it was too hot. With this, he left his well-worked breastplate in the gym, the sweat dripping and his dark-skinned light. All these details were a natural aphrodisiac for those two "Perverts".

Pretending nothing was happening, a conversation was initiated between the three of them.

-Did you prepare a good class, professor? - Asked Amelinha.

-Yes! Let's start with what article? - Asked Renato.

-I don't know... - said Amelinha.

-How about we have fun first? After you took off your shirt, I got wet! - Confessed Belinha.

-I also- Said Amelinha.

-You two are really sex maniacs! Isn't that what I love? - Said the master.

Without waiting for an answer, he took off his blue jeans showing the adductor muscles of his thigh, his sunglasses showing his blue eyes and finally his underwear showing a perfection of long penis, medium thickness and with triangular head. It was enough for the little whores to fall on top and begin to enjoy that manly, jovial body. With his help, they took their clothes off and started the preliminaries of sex.

In short, this was a wonderful sexual encounter where they experienced many new things. It was almost forty minutes of wild sex in complete harmony. In these moments, the emotion was so great that they didn't even notice the time and space. Therefore, they were infinite through God's love.

When they reached ecstasy, they rested a little on the couch. They then studied the disciplines charged by the competition. As students, the two were helpful, intelligent and disciplined, which was noted by the teacher. I'm sure they were on their way to approval.

Three hours later, they quit promising new study meetings. Happy in life, the perverted sisters went to take care of their other duties already thinking about their next adventures. They were known in the city as "The Insatiable".

Competition test

It's been a while. For about two months, the perverted sisters were dedicating themselves to the contest according to the time available. Every day that went by, they were more prepared for whatever came and went. At the same time, there were sexual encounters and in these moments they were liberated.

The test day had finally arrived. Leaving early from the capital of the hinterland, the two sisters began to walk the BR 232 highway of a total route of 250 km. On the way, they passed by the main points of the interior of the state: Pesqueira, Belo Jardim, São Caetano, Caruaru, Gravatá, Bezerros and Vitória de Santo Antão. Each of these cities had a story to tell and from their experience they absorbed it completely. How good it was to see the mountains, the Atlantic forest, the caatinga, the farms, farms, villages, small towns and to sip the clean air coming from the forests. Pernambuco was a really wonderful state!

Entering the urban perimeter of the capital, they celebrate the good realization of the Journey. Take the main avenue to the neighborhood good trip where they would perform the test. On the way, they face congested traffic, indifference from strangers, polluted air and lack of guidance. But they finally made it. They enter the respective building, identify themselves and begin the test that would last two periods. During the first part of the test, they are totally focused on the challenge of multiple choice questions. Well elaborated by the bank responsible for the event, prompted the most diverse elaborations of the two. In their view, they were doing well. When they took the break, they went out for lunch and a juice at a restaurant in front of the building. These moments were important for them to maintain their trust, relationship and friendship.

After that, they went back to the test site. Then began the second period of the event with issues dealing with other disciplines. Even without keeping the same pace, they were still very perceptive in their responses. They proved in this way that the best way to pass contests is by devoting a lot to studies. A while later, they ended their confident participation. They handed over the evidence, returned to the car, moving towards the beach located nearby.

On the way, they played, turned on the sound, commented on the race and advanced in the streets of Recife watching the illuminated streets of the capital because it was almost night. They marvel at the spectacle seen. No wonder the city is known as the "Capital of the tropics". The sun set giving the environment an even more magnificent look. How nice to be there at that moment!

When they reached the new point, they approached the shores of the sea and then launched into its cold and calm waters. The feeling provoked is ecstatic of joy, contentment, satisfaction and peace. Losing track of time, they swim till they're tired. After that, they lie on the beach in starlight without any fear or worry. Magic took hold of them brilliantly. One word to be used in this case was "Immeasurable".

At some point, with the beach almost deserted, there is an approach of two men of the girls. They try to stand up and run in the face of danger. But they are stopped by the strong arms of the boys.

—Take it easy, girls! We're not gonna hurt you! We only ask for a little attention and affection! - One of them spoke.

Faced with the mellow tone, the girls laughed with emotion. If they wanted sex, why not satisfy them? They were masters in this art. Responding to their expectations, they stood up and helped them take off their clothes. They delivered two condoms and made a striptease. It was enough to drive those two men crazy.

Falling to the ground, they loved each other in pairs and their movements made the floor shake. They allowed themselves all the sexual variations and desires of both. At this point of delivery, they didn't care about anything or anyone. For them, they were alone in the universe in a great ritual of love without prejudice. In sex, they were fully intertwined producing a power never before seen. Like instruments, they were part of a larger force in the continuation of life.

Just exhaustion forces them to stop. Fully satisfied, the men quit and walk away. The girls decide to go back to the car. They begin their journey back to their residence. Totally well, they took with them their experiences and expected good news about the contest they participated in. They certainly deserved the best luck in the world.

Three hours later, they came home in peace. They thank God for the blessings granted by going to sleep. In the other day, I was waiting for more emotions for the two maniacs.

The return of the teacher

Dawn. The sun rises early with its rays passing through the cracks of the window going to caress the faces of our dear babes. In addition, the fine morning breeze helped create mood in them. How nice it was to have the opportunity of another day with Father's blessing. Slowly, the two are getting up from their respective beds at almost the same time. After bathing, their meeting takes place in the canopy where they prepare breakfast together. It's a moment of joy, anticipation and distraction sharing experiences at incredibly fantastic times.

After breakfast is ready, they gather around the table comfortably seated on wooden chairs with a backrest for the column. While they eat, they exchange intimate experiences.

Belinha

My sister, what was that?
Amelinha
Pure emotion! I still remember every detail of the bodies of those dear cretins!
Belinha
Me too! I felt a great pleasure. It was almost extrasensory.
Amelinha
I know! Let's do these crazy things more often!
Belinha
I agree!
Amelinha
Did you like the test?
Belinha
I loved it. I'm dying to check my performance!
Amelinha
Me too!

As soon as they finished feeding, the girls picked up their cell phones by accessing the mobile internet. They navigated to the organization's page to check the feedback of the proof. They wrote it down on paper and went to the room to check the answers.

Inside, they jumped for joy when they saw the good note. They had passed! The emotion felt could not be contained right now. After celebrating a lot, he has the best idea: Invite Master Renato so that they can celebrate the success of the mission. Belinha is again in charge of the mission. She picks up her phone and calls.

Belinha
Hello?
Renato
Hi, are you okay? How are you, sweet Belle?
Belinha
Very well! Guess what just happened.
Renato

Don't tell me you....
Belinha
Yes! We passed the contest!
Renato
My congratulations! Didn't I tell you?
Belinha
I want to thank you very much for your cooperation in every way. You understand me, don't you?
Renato
I do understand. We need to set something up. Preferably at your house.
Belinha
That's exactly why I called. Can we do it today?
Renato
Yes! I can do it tonight.
Belinha
Wonder. We expect you then at eight o'clock at night.
Renato
Okay. Can I bring my brother?
Belinha
Of course !
Renato
See you later!
Belinha
See you later!

The connection ends. Looking at her sister, Belinha lets out a laugh of happiness. Curious, the other asks:
Amelinha
So what? Is he coming?
Belinha
It is all right! At eight o'clock tonight we'll be reunited. He and his brother are coming! Have you thought about Suruba?

Amelinha

Tell me about it! I'm already throbbing with emotion!

Belinha

Let there be heart! I hope it works out!

Amelinha

-It's all worked out!

The two laugh simultaneously filling the environment with positive vibrations. At that moment, I had no doubt that fate was conspiring for a night of fun for that maniac duo. They had already achieved so many stages together that they would not weaken now. They should therefore continue to idolize men as a sexual play and then discard them. That was the least race could do to pay for their suffering. In fact, no woman deserves to suffer. Or rather, almost every woman deserves no pain.

Time to get to work. Leaving the room already ready, the two sisters go to the garage where they leave in their private car. Amelinha takes Belinha to school first and then leaves for the farm office. There, she exudes joy and tells the professional news. For the approval of the competition, he receives the congratulations of all. The same thing happens to Belinha.

Later, they return home and meet again. Then begins the preparation to receive your colleagues. The day promised to be even more special.

Exactly at the scheduled time, they hear knocking at the door. Belinha, the smartest of them, gets up and answers. With firm and safe steps he puts himself in the door and opens it slowly. Upon completion of this operation, he visualize the pair of brothers. With a signal from the hostess, they enter and settle on the sofa in the living room.

Renato

This is my brother. His name is Ricardo.

Belinha

Nice to meet you, Ricardo.

Amelinha
You are welcome here!
Ricardo
I thank you both. The pleasure is all mine!
Renato
I'm ready! Can we just go to the room?
Belinha
Come on!
Amelinha
Who gets who now?
Renato
I choose Belinha myself.
Belinha
Thank you, Renato, thank you! We are together!
Ricardo
I'll be happy to stay with Amelinha!
Amelinha
You're going to tremble!
Ricardo
We'll see!
Belinha
Then let the party begin!

The men gently placed the women on the arm carrying them up to the beds located in the bedroom of one of them. Arriving at the place, they take off their clothes and fall in the beautiful furniture starting the ritual of love in several positions, exchange caresses and complicity. The excitement and pleasure were so great that the groans produced could be heard across the street scandalizing the neighbors. I mean, not so much, because they already knew about their fame.

With the conclusion from the top, the lovers return to the kitchen where they drink juice with cookies. While they eat, they chat for two hours, increasing the group's interaction. How good it was to be there learning about life and how to be happy. Contentment is being well with yourself and with the world affirming its experiences and values before others carrying the certainty of not being able to be judged by others. Therefore, the maximum they believed was "Each one is his own person".

By nightfall, they finally say goodbye. The visitors leave leaving the "Dear Pyrenees" even more euphoric when thinking about new situations. The world just kept turning towards the two confidants. May they be lucky!

End